THE MOUSE FAMILY'S MOST TERRIBLE, TERRIFYING DAY

Helping Children Cope with Terrorism Fears

Dr. Joan S. Dunphy

Illustrations by Erik DePrince

and Jessica Volinski

Small Horizons

Far Hills, New Jersey

All author royalties will be donated to Feed the Children

Library of Congress Control Number: 2002106912

Dunphy, Joan S.
        The Mouse Family's Most Terrible, Terrifying Day

ISBN: 0-88282-227-6
SMALL HORIZONS
A division of New Horizon Press
2006 2005 2004 2003 2002 / 5 4 3 2 1
Printed in the U.S.A.

Malachy Mouse woke up that mild Tuesday fall morning and felt happy. It was the second day of his second week in first grade. He no longer had butterflies in his stomach. He no longer felt lonely in the big new school. He had made two friends, Salina and Howard. His mother said he should try to make another one today. Anxious to get to school, Malachy threw the covers back. He jumped out of bed and put on his new red shirt and bright blue pants. Then he washed his face, brushed his teeth and went out to the kitchen.

"Good morning, Malachy, dear," his mother said and kissed his cheek.

"Good morning, son." His father put a plate of food in front of the little mouse.

Malachy could hardly sit still, but his mother insisted, "You must eat all your Swiss cheese and drink your milk so you'll grow up to be strong like Daddy."

"I can walk Malachy to school today Maureen, I don't have to be at work until 9:30," Malachy's father said in his deepest voice.

Malachy's mother smiled at her husband. Malachy could see she was very proud of him.

In June, the factory where Michael Mouse was a supervisor closed. Though he searched and searched for a job, he could not find any work. Finally, he had traveled to the big city, where his brother Joel lived. There Michael found a new job as Tour Director for Citi Sights. "It was," Malachy's mother had said, "a great opportunity." *Whatever that meant*, Malachy thought.

Although they were all sad to leave their cozy country cottage, his parents had told Malachy, "It will be a real adventure living in the greatest city in America." They were right. At first, they stayed with Aunt Josephine, Uncle Joel Mouse and their children. Uncle Joel worked in a restaurant, in a tall tower. You had to take the elevator to the 91st floor. It was the most wonderful restaurant Malachy had ever seen with windows all around.

On the weekends they all went sightseeing. They had already taken Malachy to see the Statue of Liberty, the Empire State Building and FAO Schwartz, the largest toy store in the world. The little mouse's eyes had grown huge with excitement and awe at all these wonderful sights.

After much searching, Malachy, his mother and father had settled into an apartment across the street from the tall towers. The offices of Citi Sights, where his father worked, were located in the basement.

"Have a good day," Malachy's mother said, "and don't forget I'm on the late shift, so you two must get your own dinners."

Malachy's mother, a nurse, had recently found a job in the emergency room of a nearby hospital. She hugged Malachy; then she gave his father a kiss and stood watching them through the cubby hole opening as they left.

Malachy's father held his son's hand tightly as they crossed the street on their way to Malachy's school. As his parents had taught him, Malachy looked up, down and all around at each corner. "Good boy, Malachy," his father said. "Someday soon you will be able to go to school by yourself." Malachy no longer felt so afraid of the tall buildings or the many people who were hurrying to their own workplaces or schools. Still, he was glad his father was close by.

A short while later, Malachy saw the red brick school building. "There it is, Dad," the little mouse pointed. Once in front they stopped and Malachy's dad bent down to kiss his son goodbye.

"Oh Daddy," Malachy said, "the kids will think I'm a baby."

His father laughed and patted Malachy on the back. "Okay then, son. Have a good day."

As Malachy began to walk away, he saw his dad wipe away a tear. "You're such a big boy," his dad said.

Malachy stiffened his back and marched straight into the school. He did not look back, so he did not see his father, hidden by a street lamp, still watching him. Walking into the classroom, he saw his two friends. They waved. Then Malachy saw a new little mouse in class. Malachy smiled and the little mouse smiled back. The teacher called out, "Good morning, class. Settle down, settle down. Please take your seats so we can begin today's lesson."

Several minutes later, when the huge boom sounded, Malachy and his classmates were looking at the blackboard where his teacher was writing the letters of the alphabet. Malachy's father had stopped for a newspaper and a coffee a few blocks away. His mother, in the apartment at Liberty Place, was sitting at her desk, reading over her notes on the patients she would tend that night. Malachy Mouse felt his heart quiver. Michael Mouse's hand trembled on the plastic coffee cup the man at the stand had just given him. Maureen Mouse felt a crick in her back, as she was thrown from her chair and landed with a thud on the floor. All of them were startled; none of them knew what that terrible, terrifying sound was.

At first, they all thought it was an earthquake. A few minutes later, there was a second, even louder boom. That was when Maureen Mouse looked out the tiny window and saw smoke pouring from the two buildings across the street.

Everyone was running down the street where Michael Mouse stood. Some were covered with soot. They yelled, "Two planes have crashed into the towers of the World Trade Center!"

At that moment, Malachy's teacher was telling the children to be calm, that the school building had to be cleared out. "Please make a straight line at the classroom door."

Malachy had never been so frightened in his life. Most of all he was frightened that he would not see his father or mother again. Nevertheless, he did what the teacher said and got into line at the door near his two friends, Salina and Howard. Next to them stood the new mouse who had just joined the class this morning. "My name is Justin," the little brown mouse said shakily. Malachy nodded and then patted the frightened looking mouse on the shoulder. "How weird," murmured Malachy, "that even on this scary day I am making a new friend."

The teachers led Malachy and the other mice children outside the school building. "Please do not be frightened. We're going to wait here with you until your parents, baby-sitters and guardians arrive to take you home," Malachy's teacher announced.

As they waited, Malachy tried to be brave, but his lip quivered. He looked around. The other little mouse faces looked worried. Malachy was worried too.

Parents and other adults started to arrive. They hugged their children and took them away. Finally, Malachy saw his mother. She was carrying a small suitcase. Then he saw his dad coming from the opposite direction. They hurried towards him. His mother put down the suitcase and hugged his father. Then they both hugged Malachy at the same time. "Mom, Dad, you're okay," Malachy cried out.

"We're fine, son. Brave firefighters, policemen and rescue workers saved many thousands. But," he said sadly, "a lot of creatures have been harmed today."

"What happened?" asked Malachy.

"Some bad people crashed airplanes into the tall towers across from our home."

"Why did they do that?" Malachy asked perplexed.

"They are very angry at our country and want to hurt it," his father said, "but Americans must show them we are strong and that creatures must talk over differences and not hurt each other."

"Are we going home now?" Malachy asked.

"I'm afraid not," Malachy's mother shook her head slowly. "Our building is filled with bad fumes and thick smoke. The firefighters came and told us we would have to stay out until they think it is safe to come back. We will have to go to Uncle Joel and Aunt Josephine's home and stay with them."

The Mouse family slowly made their way along crowded streets filled with people and soot. Each of his parents held one of Malachy's paws so he would feel more secure. When they finally reached Uncle Joel's and Aunt Josephine's apartment they were very glad to be there. They went down to the basement and knocked on the door. Aunt Josephine answered. Her eyes were swollen and red and she was crying.

"What's wrong?" Malachy's father asked.

"Joel has not come home yet. He went to work early this morning and I haven't heard from him all day. You know the restaurant where he works was at the top of one of the towers that came crashing down."

"I'll go look for him right now," Michael Mouse said

"I'll come with you, Dad," Malachy offered.

"No son, it is better if you stay here with your cousins and help your mother and Aunt Josephine. I'll come back as soon as I can."

It seemed to Malachy that many hours passed. Malachy and his cousins Carly and Dennis played games like indoor tag and Mouse, Mouse, Rat, but they kept watching the door. They hoped to see their two fathers return.

Finally Malachy's father appeared. He was alone.

"I don't have very good news, I'm afraid," he said. "No one has seen Joel since he went to work early this morning. There are many others looking for their friends and relatives. I will go back tomorrow and keep going every day after that until we find him. We shall have to wait and pray."

In the days that followed, Michael Mouse kept his word. He went to the World Trade Center site, which was now being called Ground Zero, and the hospitals and shelters in the neighboring areas everyday. He put up a picture of Uncle Joel, but like many others who were lost, Joel Mouse never came home. The family held a memorial service for Uncle Joel. All his friends and neighbors said wonderful things about him. Malachy's cousins felt very proud of their father, but they missed him very much all the same. They all were very sad and many things were confusing and frightening, especially for the children.

Life for the Mouse family changed forever after that terrible day. Malachy's school was moved to another building. Some of his classmates' parents were missing. Malachy heard the adults talking in hushed voices late into the night. They sounded upset. His father wore a worried look on his face. Malachy was afraid. Mostly he was scared that his mother and his father would get "lost" like Cousin Joel and never come back. Then what would happen to him?

Malachy began biting his tiny nails. Malachy could not sleep. He did not feel hungry. Sometimes he felt so angry he even got into fights with his best friends and Malachy's cousins were even angrier than he was. They fought with each other all the time. Malachy heard Aunt Josephine say little Dennis was having a lot of nightmares. Malachy was having nightmares, too.

When Malachy's mom and dad announced, "We'll soon be able to go back to our own home," Malachy hid under the bed.

"I don't want to go back there!" he yelled loudly and cried for a long time.

The next night, when they were sitting outside on the front steps of the building after dinner, the children saw a plane in the sky. "Look out!" little Dennis yelled. The children ran and hid behind a lamppost. Seeing how scared the children were, Michael, Maureen and Josephine decided something would have to be done about how the children were feeling.

"A lot of bad things happened on September 11," Malachy's dad said.

"Our children are frightened and angry," Aunt Josephine added.

"We have to talk to them about their fears," said Malachy's mother.

"They need to know their feelings are okay. They need to know about all the things our leaders and others are doing so our children will be safe," said Michael Mouse.

"What can we do to help our children feel better?" the three adult mice asked each other. The three mice thought and thought. Finally, they decided to take the children on a field trip to see how people were working hard to protect the country. They made a list of the places they wanted to visit.

"Tomorrow is Saturday," said Malachy's dad, "Let us talk to the children first thing in the morning and tell them about our plans for the weekend."

Bright and early the next morning, the adult mice gathered their children in the living room.

"Children," Malachy's mother said, "we know that since September 11th, you have been feeling very confused and afraid, as have we all. We want you to know that this is a good world even when bad things happen."

"But what about our daddy?" said Cousin Carly.

Aunt Josephine picked up her daughter and put Carly on her lap. "My dearest child, death is a natural part of life and something which comes to us all. That is why the time we spend together is so precious."

"Most creatures live to be very old," said Malachy's father. "However, sometimes accidents and bad things happen."

"Then, sadly, some of us, like Uncle Joel, die before our times," said Malachy's mother.

"But it may happen to you and Daddy," Malachy protested, wiping a tear away.

"Or to you, Mommy," wept Cousin Carly. "Then Dennis and I won't have a Mommy or a Daddy."

"Do not be frightened, children," said Aunt Josephine. "If something happens to any one of us grown-ups, then you would live with an aunt or uncle or your grandparents, all of whom love you."

"And it is very unlikely that these bad things will happen to us." Malachy's father added.

"But——," said Malachy.

"But if one did, you will be taken care of by those you love. We are going to talk to you later about the relatives with whom you could live," his father said, "and we will make plans together, so you will know someone will be there to care for you no matter what happens. I am sure our country will be fine and these plans won't be necessary. Remember, our president, all our soldiers, sailors, fighter pilots, police, firefighters and good friends around the world are working very hard to catch the bad people who planned this. We are going to spend time this weekend showing you some of the things our country is doing so all children will be more secure and protected."

"We have prepared backpacks for us all," said Aunt Josephine, "Quickly, eat your breakfasts, then put on your sweaters and backpacks. We will go on a little adventure to see Operation Enduring Freedom at work."

A short while later, the mice trooped out of the apartment and headed for their first stop – Ground Zero. There they saw the brave firefighters and police searching for those who had perished. Some people cheered them and the mice joined in. The adult mice read to the children the messages people had put up on walls, fences and street posts. They pointed out the candles and the flowers that so many had brought to honor those like Uncle Joel who were gone. The children petted two of the dogs that had been brought to Ground Zero to lift people's spirits. Other dogs were helping rescue workers. When the dogs licked the little mice's whiskers, the children laughed. The children even saw the picture of Uncle Joel that Malachy's father had pinned to a wall. It felt good to see the flowers and notes beneath it and know how many people cared.

Next, they all took a subway ride to the airport. Malachy's father pointed out the National Guardsmen, dressed in brown, green and white camouflage uniforms. At first, Malachy and his cousins were scared of the guards. "They have awfully big rifles," Malachy said, pointing to one.

The guardsman heard Malachy and bent down. "These guns are just to protect us all from bad people." The mice saw all the machines scanning luggage and watched as airport workers searched for problems. "Everyone is being extra careful so nothing bad will happen," Malachy's mother said.

Malachy breathed a sigh of relief. "That's good," he said.

After a picnic lunch of fruit and cheese, the mice took the airport bus back to the city.

They went to the hospital where Malachy's mother worked. She took them to the emergency room. "Here is the part of the hospital where the doctors and nurses care for people who are injured or become sick suddenly," Malachy's mother said. She showed them the machines to check people's hearts and the X-ray equipment. "I'm glad you can help so many people here, Aunt Maureen," Carly said thankfully.

Late that afternoon, the mice got on a Mousehound Bus to travel upstate where the nearest air force base was located. "We're going to stay with your Uncle Andrew and his family for the night," Aunt Josephine explained. "They are going to take us to see the military base near their cottage tomorrow."

On Sunday morning, the family gathered for a big pancake breakfast and went to a prayer service for the victims of September 11 and their loved ones. Leaders of the Catholic, Protestant, Jewish and Muslim faiths prayed with the those gathered. The pastor said, "May all the innocent beings lost on September 11th find peace with God." The rabbi added, "May God always care for us all." Malachy said his own silent prayer for children everywhere who are frightened and sad.

Afterwards, the mice headed for the air force base where they took a tour. A captain showed them members of the military marching and training to guard us at home and abroad. Then he took them to a big room. He pointed to a large screen with a lot of little black dots on it. "Those are our planes flying all the time to guard our skies." Malachy sighed. He felt relieved to know so many people were protecting his country.

Later, back at their cousins' cottage, they got ready to go back to the city. The mice were tired but excited by everything they had seen. Aboard the bus home, the three adults and children decided to make a list of things they could do for themselves and others who were worried or harmed by the bad things that had happened on September 11th. Malachy turned to his mother and said, "I know we will be tired when we get back, but could we make some of your special chocolate chip cookies? I want to bring them to the firefighters and police at Ground Zero." He turned to his father. "We could get up early and drop them there before school."

"Malachy," his mother and father said smiling, "what a good idea. We'll be happy to help you."

"I'm going to bring our list to school for Show and Tell on Monday morning," Malachy said, "so I can help other children who feel scared like I did." Then he stood up on his tiptoes to show he was "standing tall."

"I think that would be a very good thing to do." Malachy's mother patted her son's head proudly.

That night for the first time since September 11th, Malachy, his mother and father went home to 1 Liberty Plaza. After they put on their pajamas and baked the cookies, the Mouse family sat around the kitchen table drinking hot chocolate. They talked about all they had seen and how their family could continue to help others. When they went to bed, they slept very well, for they knew all over the world good creatures were working very hard to keep everyone, especially children, safe.

— THE END —

Ways Children Can Feel Safer and More Secure During These Scary Times

1. Talk to parents and teachers about how you are feeling.
2. Get plenty of sleep.
3. Play and exercise to feel better.
4. Eat nutritious foods. Never skip meals.
5. Ask teachers and adults what leaders and others are doing to make our world safe.
6. Ask adults to tell you about the brave firefighters, police, rescue workers and the military who work to protect us.
7. Do activities you enjoy.
8. Spend time with your pets and friends.
9. Ask for help from adults if you can't sleep or feel angry.
10. Spend time doing things with your family.

Things Children Can Do To Help

1. Write letters to rescue workers, service people, fire fighters and police to thank them for their bravery and hard work.
2. Write letters to the children who lost a parent telling them you appreciate and remember their parent's sacrifice.
3. Wash cars, have bake sales or sell lemonade and give the money to charity funds for the victims.
4. Donate money from your allowance to children being hurt by terrorists around the world, through charity funds like Feed the Children, Save the Children and UNICEF.

5. Help your school organize a holiday toy drive for children who lost a parent to terrorist attacks.
6. Collect clothes for families in need.
7. Hang a flag in your room.
8. Pray for the brave people who help the victims and those who are hurt or lost.
9. Pray for us all to find our way to lasting peace throughout the world.

Ways Parents, Teachers and Other Adults Can Help Children

1. Listen and talk to children about their feelings.
2. Be aware of what is being shown on television and try to limit children's viewing of disaster news.
3. Watch what you say in anger about what should be done to the terrorists. Children learn to react through what adults model.
4. Talk about the terroristic acts, why people do such things and why it is not a solution to problems.
5. Answer children's questions; do not avoid them.
6. Get on with life and maintain routines, family rules and duties.
7. Stress that it is important to take care of oneself.
8. Reassure children that you love them and that you will take care of them.
9. Stay involved as a family in each other and the world.
10. Discuss with children how they can help those who have been affected by disaster. You will build a foundation of caring and reaching out.
11. Be consistent.
12. Teach children coping skills for times when they feel angry, sad or frustrated.

13. Talk to your family doctor and get professional counseling help if needed.

14. Discuss with your children who would take care of them if you could not.

Places to Call for Counseling and Helpful Advice

National Red Cross toll-free hotline: (866) 483-4636

Red Cross hotline for families only: (866) 483-5137

The Children's Aid Society: (212) 949-2936

National Center for Victims of Crime: (800) FYI-CALL

National Organization for Victim Assistance: (800) TRY-NOVA (879-6682)

Web sites to Visit for Counseling and Helpful Advice

The Red Cross: http://www.redcross.org

The Children's Aid Society: http://www.childrensaidsociety.org

National Center for Victims of Crime: http://www.ncvc.org

National Organization for Victim Assistance: http://www.try-nova.org

American Academy of Pediatrics, "AAP Offers Advice on Communicating
    with Children About Disasters":
    http://www.aap.org/advocacy/releases/disastercomm.htm

THE SMALL HORIZONS SERIES
Written by teachers and mental health professionals teaching children:
crisis, coping, tolerance and service skills

Other Books in the Small Horizons Series:

There's a Skunk in My Bunk: Helping Children Learn Tolerance
By Joseph T. McGann, Psy.D.; art by Thomas Gerlach
48 pages/26 color illustrations; ISBN: 0-88282-214-4 (pb), $12.95
To be released December 2002

My Stick Family: Helping Children Cope With Divorce
By Natalie June Reilly and Brandi J. Pavese
48 pages/26 color illustrations; ISBN: 0-88282-207-1 (pb), $12.95

I'm So Angry, I Could Scream: Helping Children Deal With Anger
By Laura Fox, M.A.; art by Chris Sabatino
48 pages/26 color illustrations; ISBN: 0-88282-185-7 (pb), $12.95

*The Boy Who Sat By the Window: Helping Children Cope With Violence
By Chris Loftis; art by Catherine Gallagher
52 pages/24 color illustrations; ISBN: 0-88282-147-4 (pb), $12.95

*The Special Raccoon: Helping a Child Learn About Handicaps and Love
By Kim Carlisle
42 pages/20 color illustrations; ISBN: 0-88282-096-6 (pb), $9.95

The Words Hurt: Helping Children Cope With Verbal Abuse
By Chris Loftis; art by Catherine Gallagher
46 pages/20 color illustrations; ISBN: 0-88282-132-6 (pb), $9.95

*Up and Down the Mountain: Helping Children Cope With Parental Alcoholism
By Pamela Leib Higgins; art by Gail Zawacki
48 pages/26 color illustrations; ISBN: 0-88282-133-4 (pb), $8.95

* †The Empty Place: A Child's Guide Through Grief
By Roberta Temes, Ph.D.; art by Kim Carlisle
42 pages/25 black & white illustrations; ISBN: 0-88282-118-0 (pb), $8.95

Parental Council Ltd. Selections
†A McNaughton Book

For information on ordering any of the above books, call the New Horizon Press book order department at 1-800-533-7978 or send check or money order to New Horizon Press, P.O. Box 669, Far Hills, NJ 07931. Please include the book title, ISBN# and quantity plus $2.00 shipping and handling for the first book and $.25 for each additional book. New Jersey residents add applicable sales tax. Please allow 4-6 weeks for delivery. Visit us on the web: www.newhorizonpressbooks.com

Small Horizons is an imprint of New Horizon Press